SBN 361 01395 7
Published 1969 by
PURNELL, London W. 1
Copyright © 1968 and 1969 by
WALT DISNEY PRODUCTIONS
All Rights Reserved
Printed in Italy by
Officine Grafiche A. Mondadori Editore
Verona

Walt Disney

Bambi

PURNELL
London, W.1

BAMBI came into the world in the middle of a forest thicket. The little, hidden thicket was scarcely big enough for the new baby and his mother.

But the magpie soon spied him there.

"What a beautiful baby!" she cried. And away she flew to spread the news to all the other animals of the forest.

Her chattering soon brought dozens of birds and animals to the thicket. The rabbits came hurrying; the squirrels came scurrying. The robins and bluebirds fluttered and flew.

At last even the old owl woke up from his long day's sleep.

"Who, who?" the owl said sleepily, hearing all the commotion.

"Wake up, Friend Owl!" a rabbit called. "It's happened! The young Prince is born!"

"Everyone's going to see him," said the squirrels. "You come, too."

With a sigh the owl spread his wings and flew off towards the thicket. There he found squirrels and rabbits and birds peering through the bushes at a doe and a little spotted fawn.

The fawn was Bambi, the new Prince of the Forest.

"Congratulations," said the owl, speaking for all the animals. "This is quite an occasion. It isn't often that a Prince is born in the forest."

The doe looked up. "Thank you," she said quietly. Then with her nose she gently nudged her sleeping baby until he lifted his head and looked around.

She nudged him again, and licked him reassuringly. At last he pushed up on his thin legs, trying to stand.

"Look! He's trying to stand up already!" shouted one of the little rabbits, Thumper by name. "He's awfully wobbly, though, isn't he?"

"Thumper!" the mother rabbit exclaimed, pulling him back. "That's not a pleasant thing to say!"

The new fawn's legs were not very steady, it was true, but at last he stood beside his mother. Now all the animals could see the fine white spots on his red-brown coat, and the sleepy expression on his soft baby face.

The forest around him echoed with countless small voices. A soft breeze rustled the leaves about the thicket. And the watching birds and animals whispered among themselves. But the little fawn did not listen to any of them. He only knew that his mother's tongue was licking him softly, washing and warming him. He nestled closer to her, and closed his sleepy eyes.

Quietly the animals and birds slipped away through the forest, back to their homes.

Thumper the rabbit was the last to go. He couldn't take his eyes off the baby fawn.

"What are you going to name the young Prince?" he asked.

"I'll call him Bambi," the mother answered.

"Bambi," Thumper repeated. "Bambi. That's a good name. Good-bye, Bambi." And he hopped away after his sisters.

Bambi was not a sleepy baby for long. Soon he was following his mother down the narrow forest paths, still a little shaky on his spindly legs. Bright flowers winked from beneath the leaves. Prickly branches tickled his legs as he passed. Bambi stared at them in silence.

Squirrels and chipmunks looked up and called, "Good morning, young Prince."

Opossums, hanging upside down by their long tails from a tree branch, said, "Hello, Prince Bambi."

The fawn looked at them all with huge, wondering eyes. But he still did not say a word.

Finally, as Bambi and his mother reached a little clearing in the forest, they met Thumper and his family. They were playing a game amongst themselves.

"Hi, Bambi," said Thumper. "Come on and play."

"Yes, let's play," Thumper's sister cried. And away they hopped, over branches and hillocks and tufts of grass.

It did not take Bambi long to understand the game, and soon he began to jump and run on his stiff, spindly legs.

Thumper jumped over a log and his sisters followed.

"Come on, Bambi," Thumper called. "Hop over the log."

Bambi ran at the log and jumped, but not far enough. He fell with a plop on top of the log, legs dangling over either side.

"Too bad," said Thumper. "You'll do better next time."

Bambi untangled his legs and stood up again. But still he did not speak. Thumper was disappointed. He could not think of any game that would please the baby prince enough to make him try and say something.

Still, Thumper decided to do his best. He bounded along, in and out of the trees and round and round the bushes and wherever he went, Bambi followed on his long, unsteady legs. Thumper's sisters frisked about Bambi, encouraging him.

"Come on, Bambi," they said. "Talk to us."

But Bambi just looked at them with his huge, brown eyes and said nothing.

Soon they came to a branch with a family of birds sitting on it. Bambi stopped prancing along and stared at them.

"Those are birds, Bambi," Thumper told him. "Birds."

"Bir-d," Bambi said slowly. The young Prince had spoken his first word!

Thumper and his sisters were all excited, and Bambi himself was pleased. He repeated the word over and over to himself.

"Bir-d," he said. "Bird, bird."

"That's right, Bambi," chirped the birds. "How clever you are, for such a very young prince."

"Bird," replied Bambi.

Soon they left the bird family and went on their way again. Bambi was very pleased with himself, and each time a bird flew past he cried out "Bird!"

Thumper and his sisters were once more playing their game of jumping over every low branch, hillock and clump of grass they could see. Bambi joined in, and quickly grew much better at it. He was beginning to be able to manage those long, spindly legs of his now. In a short time, he could actually leap higher than the rabbits. Thumper was delighted, and laughed to see Bambi's astonished face when he found how easily he could sail through the air. He kept finding higher and higher things for Bambi to jump over.

"Follow me, Bambi!" he cried as he bounded along.

Then Bambi saw something bright yellow fluttering across his path, and stopped to watch it.

"Bird, bird," he said.

"No, Bambi," said Thumper. "That's not a bird. That's a butterfly."

"But-terfly?" said Bambi.

The butterfly disappeared into a clump of yellow flowers. Bambi bounded toward them happily.

"Butterfly!" he cried.

"No, Bambi," said Thumper. "Not butterfly. *Flower*."

Thumper pushed his nose into the flowers and sniffed. Bambi did the same, but suddenly he drew back in surprise. His nose had touched something warm and furry.

Out from the bed of flowers came a small black head with two shining black eyes that stared at the fawn.

"Flower!" said Bambi.

The black eyes twinkled. As the little animal stepped out of the flowers, the white stripe down his black furry back glistened in the sun.

Thumper the rabbit was laughing so hard that he could scarcely speak. He rolled around on the grass, choking and spluttering.

"That's not a flower," gasped Thumper when he could draw breath. "That's a skunk."

"Flower," repeated Bambi.

"I don't care," said the skunk. "The young Prince is welcome to call me Flower if he wants to. I don't mind."

"Flower," Bambi repeated.

So Flower, the skunk, got his name.

One morning Bambi and his mother walked down a new path. The trees gradually thinned out as they walked along and it grew lighter and lighter. Soon the trail ended in a tangle of bushes and vines, and Bambi could see a great, bright, open space spread out before them.

What a lot of room for running and leaping and having fun! Bambi wanted to bound out there to play in the sunshine, but his mother stopped him. "Wait," she said. "You must never run out on the meadow without making quite sure it is safe."

She took a few slow, careful steps forward. She listened and sniffed in all directions. Then she called, "It's all right. You can come out, Bambi."

Bambi bounded out. He felt so good and so happy that he leaped into the air again and again and again. For the meadow was the most beautiful and exciting place he had ever seen.

His mother dashed forward and showed him how to race and play in the tall grass. Bambi ran after her. He felt as if he were flying. Round and round they raced in great circles. At last his mother stopped and stood still catching her breath. Bambi had a rest too, but soon he wanted to play again.

Then Bambi set out by himself to explore the meadow. Soon he spied his little friend the skunk, sitting quietly in the shade of some blossoms.

"Good morning, Flower," said Bambi.

"Good morning, Bambi," said Flower.

And he found Thumper and his sisters busily nibbling sweet clover.

"Try some, Bambi," said Thumper.

So Bambi did, and enjoyed it.

Suddenly a big green frog popped out of the clover patch and

startled Bambi. The frog hopped over to a meadow pond. Bambi had not seen the pond before, so he hurried over for a closer look.

As the fawn came near, the frog hopped into the water.

Where could he have gone? Bambi wondered. So he bent down to look into the clear water of the pond. As the ripples cleared, Bambi jumped back. For he saw another fawn down there in the water, looking out at him!

"Don't be frightened, Bambi," his mother told him. "You are just seeing yourself in the water."

So Bambi looked once more. This time he saw *two* fawns looking back at him! There couldn't possibly be two of him! He jumped back again, but as he lifted his head he saw that it was true—there was another little fawn standing beside him!

"Hello," she said.

Bambi backed away shyly and ran to his mother, where she was quietly eating grass beside another doe. Bambi leaned against her and peered out at the other little fawn, who had followed him and was looking at him in a friendly way.

"Don't be afraid, Bambi," his mother said. "This is little Faline, your cousin, and this is your Aunt Ena. Can't you say hello to them?"

"Hello, Bambi," said the two deer. But Bambi did not say a word. He just stood peering out at them.

"You have been wanting to meet other deer," his mother reminded him. "Well, Aunt Ena and Faline are deer just like us. Now can't you speak to them?"

"Hello," whispered Bambi in a small, small voice.

"Come and play, Bambi," said Faline, who wasn't at all shy. She leaned forward and licked his face.

Bambi dashed away as fast as he could run, and Faline raced after him. They almost flew over that meadow.

Up and down they chased each other. Over the little hillocks they raced, and Faline could leap just as high as Bambi.

When they stopped, all topsy-turvy and breathless, they were good friends.

Then they walked quietly side by side on the bright meadow, each quite happy in the other's company.

One morning, Bambi woke up shivering with cold, and when he looked out of the thicket, everything was white.

"It's snow, Bambi," his mother said. "Go out in it."

Bambi stepped out on to the snow very cautiously. His feet sank deep into it, and the sun glittered brightly on the whiteness. White snow stars came whirling down. He was delighted.

Then he saw Thumper, sitting on top of the pond!

"Come on, Bambi!" Thumper shouted. "Look! The water's quite stiff!" He thumped with one foot against the solid ice. "You can even slide on it. Watch!"

Thumper took a run and slid swiftly across the pond. Bambi tried it, too, but his legs shot out from under him and down he crashed on the hard ice. That was not so much fun.

"Let's play something else," Bambi suggested, when he had carefully pulled himself to his feet again. "Where's Flower?"

"I think I know," said Thumper.

He led Bambi to the doorway of a deep burrow. Inside, sleeping on a bed of withered flowers, lay the little skunk.

"Wake up, Flower!" Bambi called.

"Is it spring yet?" Flower asked sleepily, half opening his eyes.

"No, it's winter," Bambi said. "What are you doing?"

"Hibernating," the little skunk replied. "Flowers always sleep in the winter, you know."

"I'm sleepy, too," yawned Thumper. "I'll see you later, Bambi."

Left alone, Bambi wandered sadly back to the thicket.

"Don't fret, Bambi," his mother said. "Spring will come again."

So Bambi went to sleep beside his mother in the snug, warm thicket, and dreamed of the happy games that he and his friends would play in the wonderful spring to come.